FUZZY RABBIT
SAVES CHRISTMAS

By Rosemary Billam
Pictures by Vanessa Julian-Ottie

A Random House PICTUREBACK®

Random House ⌂ New York

For Charlie and Otis
R.B.

First American Edition, 1991. Text copyright © 1990 by Rosemary Billam. Illustrations copyright © 1990 by Vanessa Julian-Ottie. All rights reserved under International and Pan-American Copyright Conventions. Published in the United States by Random House, Inc., New York. Originally published in Great Britain as *Alpaca Saves Christmas* by William Collins Sons & Co., London, in 1990. This edition is published by arrangement with William Collins Sons & Co.

Library of Congress Cataloging-in-Publication Data
Billam, Rosemary. Fuzzy Rabbit Saves Christmas / by Rosemary Billam ; illustrated by Vanessa Julian-Ottie.   p.   cm. — (A Random House pictureback) Summary: Ellen and Robert leave Fuzzy Rabbit under the tree on Christmas Eve and he is thus on hand to save the holiday when Santa falls asleep in their sitting room. ISBN 0-679-80460-9. [1. Christmas — Fiction.   2. Toys — Fiction.   3. Rabbits — Fiction.] I. Julian-Ottie, Vanessa, ill.   II. Title.   PZ7.B494Fx 1991   [E]—dc20   89-77934   CIP   AC

Manufactured in the United States of America   10 9 8 7 6 5 4 3 2 1

It was Christmas Eve. Ellen and Robert gazed at their Christmas tree as it sparkled in the firelight.

"Santa Claus is coming tonight," Ellen told Robert for the hundredth time.

Fuzzy Rabbit looked up at the fairy on top of the tree.

"Lucky thing," he thought. "She'll see Santa when he comes."

Robert put some cookies on a plate in case Santa was hungry, and Ellen poured a glass of milk and left it on the mantel in case he was thirsty as well.

Then they all sang Christmas carols around the tree, until Daddy said it was time Fuzzy went to bed.

Ellen sat Fuzzy on her pillow while she took her bath. Fuzzy could hear her singing in the bathroom. He felt warm and happy.

At bedtime the children hung their stockings at the end of their beds.

Ellen had made a small stocking especially for Fuzzy. What a lovely surprise!

"I'm not going to sleep till Santa comes," said Robert.

"Santa won't come until you are fast asleep," said Mommy.

"Look out the window and see if he's coming now," said Robert. But there was only a group of carolers under the streetlight.

Ellen was tired, but sleep wouldn't come.

Fuzzy couldn't sleep either…

and Robert was wide awake. He stared at his empty stocking. Suddenly, he heard a noise outside.

"Sleigh bells!" he said. He tiptoed over to the window and looked out.

"It's only a car," said Ellen.

The front doorbell rang and there were voices and laughter in the hall. Robert scurried out to the landing and peered down.

Soon he heard Mommy and Daddy coming upstairs. He ran back to bed and pretended to be asleep when they peeped into the room. Only Fuzzy had his eyes open. Robert kept absolutely still till he was sure that Mommy and Daddy were in bed. He had decided that the best way to see Santa Claus was to go downstairs and wait in the living room.

"Come on, Fuzzy," he said. "We're going downstairs."
"I'd much rather stay in bed," thought Fuzzy Rabbit.

The house was very quiet and the stairs creaked. The only light came from the streetlight outside. Fuzzy clung on to Robert as they crept downstairs.

Robert opened the door to the living room with a little click. The curtains were drawn and it was very dark. He could just make out the shape of the tree with shadows all around it. He bent down to switch on the Christmas tree lights...and dropped Fuzzy among the presents.

Just then Robert heard footsteps in the hall, and he quickly hid behind the curtain. He held his breath, but it was only Ellen.

"What are you doing down here?" she whispered, taking his arm. "It's very late. Let's go back to bed. We must be asleep before Santa comes."

They tiptoed upstairs, forgetting to switch off the lights on the Christmas tree.

"What about me?" thought Fuzzy.

After a while he sat up—and couldn't believe his eyes. He blinked and looked again.

There was Santa Claus with his sack. He stopped, turned around, and looked straight at Fuzzy. Then he smiled a great big beaming smile.

"Well, well," he said. "I didn't expect to see you. Why aren't you tucked in bed?"

Santa put his sack on the floor and sat down in the armchair. He helped himself to the milk and cookies.

"Very good," he said. He yawned, leaned back in the chair, and nodded off to sleep.

"Oh dear," thought Fuzzy. "What about all the other boys and girls who are waiting for him?"

Fuzzy sat and watched Santa snoring gently in the armchair. The clock in the hall struck one. Fuzzy tried to nudge him awake, but it didn't work, so he tugged at his beard.

Santa Claus woke with a start. He looked at the clock on the mantel.

"Bless me," he said. "I must hurry." He took Fuzzy upstairs and put him back in Ellen's bed.

Fuzzy lay there and watched as Santa filled the stockings with little presents. Then Santa kissed Fuzzy good night. It must have been a magic kiss, because Fuzzy went straight to sleep and didn't remember another thing.

In the morning Ellen and Robert woke up early. "He's been here! He's been here!" shouted Robert, waking up Fuzzy, who was still sound asleep. In Fuzzy's own little stocking Ellen found a hat and scarf which fitted him perfectly. Mommy came to the door.

"Merry Christmas, darlings," she said.

"Santa came," said Robert.

"So I see," said Mommy. "Aren't you lucky? He must have been very hungry, because he ate all the cookies and drank all the milk."

"So he did," thought Fuzzy. "And nobody knows I was there too, and that I even pulled his beard!"